Wardenclyffe

GREGG CUNNINGHAM

Available from Black Hare Press

SHORT READS
WARDENCLYFFE by GREGG CUNNINGHAM
HADES 11 by PAUL WARMERDAM
BLOOD AND SILK by ZOEY XOLTON
AS ABOVE, SO BENEATH by JOSHUA D. TAYLOR
THE RISE OF THE GREAT OLD ONE by JASMINE
JARVIS
DEAD MAN WALKING by DAVID GREEN
CHRYSALIS by KIMBERLY REI
MOUNT TERROR by E.L. GILES
HELL HATH NO FURY by CHISTO HEALY
THE RECKONING by STEPHANIE SCISSOM
THEY by G. ALLEN WILBANKS
THE SPIRIT OF RODEO by BETH W. PATTERSON
THE BOOKWORM by ANDREAS HORT and L.T.
EMERY
THIS HIDEOUS JOY by JONATHAN INBODY
THE CORONOR by J. MOTOKI
SPIRITUS EX MACHINA by G. ALLEN WILBANKS

UNDERGROUND
THE RETURN by GABRIELLA BALCOM
UNDERGROUND by STEVEN STREETER
WHISPERS IN THE DARK by K.B. ELIJAH
SWIRLING DARKNESS by SAM M. PHILLIPS
THE GATE TO THE UNDERWORLD by E.L. GILES
THOSE OF THE LIGHT by NICOLA CURRIE
TIME'S ABYSS by JAMES PYLES
UNDERWORLD GAMES by JONATHAN D. STIFFY
PLACE OF CAVES by CHARLOTTE O'FARRELL
AFTER THE FALL by STEPHEN HERCZEG
BEYOND HUMAN by MATHEW CLARKE
THE FALL OF PACIFICA by M. SYDNOR JR.

For Giulia,

I told you this would rock!

Muskie, you da' man!

Many thanks, Black Hare Press.

x
Gregg, March 2020

After receiving my battle orders from the King of England himself, I, Swarley Paxmore, Captain of the 1st King's Dragoon Guards, would lead the cavalry charge through the beastly battlefront and make haste for Liverpool. From there, we would set sail on a commandeered ship, diverted from Belfast, bound for New York.

So, with nothing more than the bloody uniforms on our backs, our Enfield rifles at the ready, and a grubby scouting map directing us safely through the enemy-occupied areas now scattered throughout the English countryside, we were to make haste over treacherous ground to the world's most elegant military transport ship moored within the docklands of Liverpool.

From there, our sea voyage onboard the Titanic would take us across the Atlantic Ocean where we would eventually make our landfall in Manhattan; rendezvousing with America's President Theodore Roosevelt, to assist in his fight against whatever terror Nikola Tesla's preposterous invention had unleashed on Long Island.

However, just as the king's orders were being received by military commanders, the electrified skies above Blackpool were torn open again, with even more of the dastardly beasts invading from another realm. I feared all would be lost before we could even reach the sanctuary of the Titanic—the finest ship ever to set sail from Great Britannia's shores, let alone cross the Atlantic Ocean—and join Roosevelt's gathering forces.

Who could have dreamed up such fantastical nightmares? Who of us could ever imagine that, in the year of our lord, nineteen hundred and twelve, we would be fighting such devilish witchcraft the likes of which only Edgar Poe could dream up for one of his elite poetry reading nights?

During my many campaigns, I can say hand on heart that I had never witnessed such brutality and downright butchery than that seen during the siege on Blackpool Tower. Putrid bodies lay festering in the abandoned promenade streets, stripped of both their humanity and uniform as they lay torn to pieces. Many of those pitiful corpses, missing limbs, and rotting in darkening pools of tacky blood infested with flies and bulging maggots.

Frightful crows, wary of the stray dogs cowering in the shadows, fed eagerly upon the exposed fleshy parts of the deceased, left to rot by the horrendous flying beasts.

Those who remained in the rubble of the dwellings overlooking the cobbled streets huddled for heat around candles that flickered weakly behind torn, pathetic curtains and fed on the scraps they had scavenged from the dead.

It took over a dozen of our artillery squadrons, and several hundred men, to blast the nesting demon creatures from the steel tower construction that loomed high over Blackpool. Even then, on our first call to arms, with the Howitzer shells exploding around us and the horrendous wailing that began piercing our ears, we doubted we could hold the blighters off for very long.

I found out during the battle that the god-awful wailing we were hearing was none other than the blasted Highland Fusiliers' marching band. They reinforced our front line with their retched bagpipes groaning away as my men and I fought the winged demons swooping from their nests high upon the ominous steel tower that overlooked the beachy head.

We watched on as those circling beasts, conjured from another realm, plucked the unlucky buggers from the sandbagged fox holes without mercy or warrant, before flying off into a night sky that had been transformed into some hellish nightmare, with swirling clouds of green and blue gases lighting up the city like a freakish northern aurora borealis light show.

This monstrosity of a tower that was, until last week, a viewing gallery for the public to visit, had become a travesty of science, a monument of utter stupidity—a tower now used by scientists to harness the electrical power held within our skies.

Zeppelin warships made long, lazy loops in the sky above as search light beams scoured the rooftops for what some imbeciles were ludicrously describing as dragons, for heaven's sake. I had never heard such balderdash, well not until I too set eyes upon the winged beasts, myself.

Gunfire and screams filled the streets as petrified mutton shunters ran from doorway to doorway, blowing their police whistles and demanding the public flee, all the while ducking frantically as the beasts swooped down from above.

I counted at least one hundred of these prehistoric devils circling Blackpool's electrified tower as it glowed with the most amazing electrical discharge I had ever witnessed. It had been converted into one huge electronic resonator; a reservoir built to harness the huge forks of lightning that seemed to strike down from the heavens, only to be devoured by the metal sphere caged on the top. From several hundred feet below that damned structure, we all felt the static discharge, our teeth vibrating vigorously in our gums.

I watched nurses risking their lives as they

tended to the bloodied men who had been torn apart on the streets by these huge ancient beasts, the likes of which I had only seen illustrated within the bindings of tacky penny press novels.

I also witnessed Sergeant Major Smith shooting nine of the winged buggers out of the sky with my very own eyes as they swooped down on our courageous men and women.

We congratulated his marksmanship on the promenade with a shared rolled cheroot over the bloody remains of one such demon, where we posed for a heliograph taken by a reporter from the London Gazette. I stood upon the beast's head, measuring almost two strides wide, while Smithy measured its huge wingspan. I might add that all the artillery boys from Company C only managed a few more kills the entire night of fighting than just myself and Smithy.

I had the good fortune to hunt with the president in Africa several years back and found him quite the sharpshooter. I would imagine the old Bull Moose over the water would likely be hunting these beasts for his own personal collection of wildlife mounted on his lodge wall. Smithy put the president's musket sharpshooting down to nothing more than good judgement and rifle maintenance. He would often tell me this over a brandy as he caressed his Enfield like he was rubbing up one of the aforementioned nurses from the Red Cross tents.

Once the battle for Blackpool was won, our orders were to leave the Yorkshire regiments and make for the Docklands of Liverpool, on our king's command. Things seemed far worse for poor old Teddy over the pond, and the king had promised his closest ally an army to help the crusade against whatever it was that had seeped from the lightning cracks in the skies over *their* shores.

We left in haste, like the looters who had stripped the shopkeepers of their goods, scattering broken beer bottles and fine brandy casks all over the thoroughfares as they fled empty-handed. It broke my heart to see such good brandy being wasted in the guttering like that, so I asked Smithy to liberate several bottles of Cognac for the journey.

We also took with us around one thousand men and most of the horses that would eventually join up with the rest of the surviving regiments onboard the ships bound for America. The Red Cross fillies followed in convoy, with the bagpipe-playing hooligans bringing up the rear. The Howitzers from the artillery and the Yorkshire Regiment remained to fight off the beasts in Blackpool.

After a bloody overnight ride through the countryside, the 1st King's Dragoon Guards charged our exhausted horses up the dockland ramps towards the hull of the *Titanic* as we fought off the flying beasts with nothing more than our bloody ceremonial swords; our ammunition had depleted much earlier than we anticipated. One out of every three riders had been picked from their mounts like petrified mice scrambling through the wheat fields of the Yorkshire Dales.

As my mount, Betsy—named after my dear mother—and I traversed the docks, the soldiers already on the ship's deck above fired indiscriminately into the feeding frenzy, watching us gallop the length of the docks as if we were riding for the King's Cup Steeplechase at Aintree. We saved as many of the nurses, cooks, and volunteers as we could, but alas, most of the brave Scots and their wailing bagpipes were left behind…on my orders.

Well, could you blame me? I couldn't understand a bloody word they were saying, not to mention the blasted wailing of their bagpipes.

Besides, they could take care of themselves.

Orders to cast off were swift, those left behind made futile efforts to jump from the dock and cling onto whatever footholds they could manage as the *Titanic* was cut from its moorings and slowly slipped away from the carnage and into the night.

Liverpool burned under a cloud of ash as the new occupiers of Britannia circled the embers of a fallen empire, a land now slowly being engulfed by the Devil himself.

We could only watch on as the exodus of Zeppelins above were picked off, one by one, by the winged serpents of hell, eager to make our land their own. We fought on into the night. Smithy and I were absolutely trounced, but it was only when we were a good couple of miles from the shore, did the beasts yield, allowing us to finally rest while the nurses tended to the wounded.

Inside the *Titanic*, soldiers crammed into the opulent cabins like tightly packed sardines in brine tins, with scarcely little room to lay on the finely woven carpets, let alone sprawl on the majestic four-poster beds. I, however, managed to secure a bunk, with only four of us sharing, after some blustering from one of the ship's stewards who tried to pull rank over my men. I gave him a ruddy good bollocking and sent him on his way.

The nurses were just as exhausted as the rest of us. I offered one of the young ladies some recuperation and a bit of *how's yer father* back in my quarters, but she declined, saying she would rather sleep with the horses in the stables...much to Smithy's amusement. I vowed to make it my goal to have the thighs of one these fine nurses wrapped around me and tucked up in one of those four-poster beds by the end of the trip and Smithy bet me a packet of his cheroots I wouldn't have a snowball's chance in hell. Didn't he remember his lesson from Dusseldorf? Never bet against the great Swarley Paxmore.

The ship's captain estimated over ten thousand

souls were aboard the *Titanic* when she left the burning shores of England, filled to the brim with Regiments from the four corners of Great Britannia, including many badly wounded. I, however, refused to yield to the Lord's calling just yet, having come close to death's icy touch on many a battlefield melee. I had once again survived obliteration, this time by those hellish, swarming winged demons.

I mean, how much worse could America actually be?

Our king, thankfully, had survived the Blackpool carnage, having evaded capture and was currently flying in the lead Zeppelin squadron formation above the *Titanic*, and we all now traversed across the North Atlantic Ocean together. The flotilla was now under the command of our Lord of Admiralty on board the lead vessel, HMS *Fearless,* a young man that went by the name of Churchill. He asserted his authority quickly, commanding the remaining ships in our fleet, which consisted of several ironclad frigates and other vessels mingling alongside the *Titanic*'s own sister ship, the *Olympic*, which limped alongside the HMS *Fearless* as we made for the call to arms by our American Allies.

Theodore Roosevelt, now serving his third term, had sent his condolences but ordered what remained of his Asiatic fleet back to Manhattan Island, with assurances from our king that Great Britannia would fight alongside the Americans in defeating this horrendous new winged foe that had been conjured from Teslas failed experiments on Long Island.

Word was, that President Roosevelt had pleaded for any nation able to, to set sail and aid them in their own battles with the creatures. It seemed something had gone terribly wrong with Nikola Tesla's worldwide experiment to align these hefty steel towers around the globe to harness the power of the Electro current. I was rather bemused by the whole thing, finding the idea—this *experiment*—ludicrous, to say the least.

Whatever madness had been unleased on Great Britannia's public, had also been released in America's own backyard, with even more catastrophic results.

The small remainder of horses still fit to ride were corralled in the cramped storage bays below and exercised around the deck as often as possible. I myself, ensured Betsy got her daily walk around the promenade deck—much to the amusement of the other men of the many regiments now occupying ghetto-like areas around the *Titanic*. It also seemed to tickle the nurses as they watched me flex my authority with the stewards, who seemed livid that I would be marking the fine mahogany wooden decks with Betsy's foot irons.

I simply waved them on their way, cursing at

the fact I still hadn't had any damn luck wooing any of our Red Cross darlings.

After roll call, I sat with Smithy on the deck. With my rifle raised, I watched the few remaining Zeppelin airships meander overhead. I was still able to see the glow of Nikola Tesla's retched Blackpool Tower on the horizon as it continued to crackle and hum above our coastline. Statically discharged fingers of lightning bolts continued to reach up high into the night sky, like a distant monsoon burning fiercely, lit by a menacing blue electrical glow.

"Damn it, Smithy!" cursed I. "They should never have turned those godforsaken electrical contraptions on!"

Sergeant Major Smith shrugged as he opened his tabloid paper with a shake.

"Mr Paxmore, sir, if I may?" Smithy chuckled, turning to me as he cleared his throat. Opening last week's newsprint, he began reading thusly.

"...Nikola Tesla, a sorcerer of magneto, had informed the world that this would be man's greatest achievement, access to free electricity for every human on earth, to further man's technological advancement and gain their understanding of how the universe works. To increase our intellect and further our knowledge of the essence of life itself. Once these towers that reach into the heavens are activated, they shall create an immense worldwide net able to circumnavigate the skies and recover the full electrical energy potential within."

"Balderdash, Smithy!" I scoffed at just how little the scientific gentry knew of the modern horrors they were unleashing. "That man is a buffoon of the highest order. Why Roosevelt let him proceed with his god-awful experiments is beyond me. Take a look at that horizon and tell me what wondrous understandings of the universe you see?"

Smithy turned but said nothing. As he knocked

the ash from his pipe against his deckchair, we sat in silence together watching the skies, realising that chaos was now ruling Britannia.

"Another brandy, sir?" says he, finally, lifting the bottle of fine 1893 Cognac he had recovered from the Blackpool looters.

"Rude not to, my good man," says I, handing the fellow my battered mug.

"For king and country!" we cheered, knocking our mugs together and sinking the fine apéritif.

"ICEBERG!"

The words echoed in the frozen darkness as we woke shivering from our broken slumber.

"ICEBERG, DEAD AHEAD!"

Some of us guarding the starboard side stood up and peered over the handrails into the darkness of the frothing waters below, searching for the iceberg in the gloom. Smithy had discovered the stockroom in the dance hall area the previous evening, and my men had partaken in a few too many white wine spritzers as some even danced along to those dreadful bagpipes. Other hungover soldiers sighed, rolling over under their blankets, unafraid as the nurses walked around checking on their wounds.

This was, after all, the *Titanic*—the unsinkable ship.

I must admit to having concerns. Ten thousand souls on board and barely enough life rafts for a fraction of them. We watched as silence quickly followed, the ship's engines groaning beneath us, each of us gasping and holding our icy breath, waiting for the impending impact.

All of a sudden, out of the frozen depths ahead appeared one solitary bobbing icecap, quietly waiting for its prey.

It poked out from the water, barely visible, but I wondered just how much of the icy menace was hidden beneath the murky sea. I pondered, inhaling slowly on my cheroot as the smoke vented into the chilled air, before turning to my right-hand man.

"I think they ought to slow this bugger of a ship

down a notch, don't you, Smithy? Who knows what dangers lurk under these waters?"

Smithy concurred, rubbing his temples as we watched another iceberg emerge from the gloom. He was a man of few words, my Sergeant Major—more a man of action, which suited me fine. The young nurse who'd shunned my advances earlier in the evening, passed us by again, nodded and held out a damp towel to attend to my hangover.

She smiled as I waved her on with a charming, yet smutty, wink, perusing her over as she walked on by. I caught a waft of last night's delightful perfume before I returned my attention to the churning sea. I watched as another iceberg appeared, this one of similar size to the first, then another quickly followed. I counted four of them, breaking the water and rising slowly on our starboard side as the warning cries began again.

"ICEBERG!"

At first, my eyes saw only the wake of the ship as we sliced past the icebergs, small insignificant pieces of flotsam that could inflict only superficial damage to her hull.

But as they rose from the frothing waters, I gasped in realisation, and stepped back from the melee of soldiers peering over the handrail. What I was seeing was no iceberg.

"What on God's green earth is that?" the Sergeant Major growled beside me.

It was Blackpool all over again.

I watched as the four prehistoric dagger-like ice plates broke from the water, shimmering in the moonlight like monolithic scutes contouring a crocodile's back.

The huge shimmering beast that swam alongside our hull, rose from the frothing sea, slowly reaching up, and sliced at the hull of our ship with what appeared to be huge frozen talons, tearing at the panelling, rivet by rivet. Loud screeching filled my ears as the beast's head emerged and let out an almighty roar. My fellow cavalry men stumbled back in shock as the *Titanic* shuddered. I, however, raised my rifle and began firing at the beast's contorting back without hesitation.

"Good god, Paxmore! The thing is almost one hundred yards long!" Smithy exclaimed.

"I'll say!" says I.

I could see its tail thrashing behind its immense body, being used as a crude rudder, but unlike the flying beasts that attacked us in Liverpool, I could see no wings on this demon. Judging by the way it opened the hull up with its talons, I was convinced that it could do us just as much, if not more, damage than those flying monstrosities that attacked our Zeppelin squadrons over Goodison Park.

I turned to Smithy as the blasted thing began screeching out again.

"Quit dilly-dallying, Smithy, and grab your bloody weapon!"

"For king and country, sir!" says he, reloading his Enfield rifle and taking aim.

The *Titanic* shuddered once more. This time the night sky was lit up by a barrage of shells fired from HMS *Fearless*, now steaming full speed for the intruder attempting to climb aboard our vessel. I watched as Churchill's command veered port bound and changed course directly into the path of the *Titanic* as the beast thrust its claws deeper into the panelling of the hull. Explosions from the coal bunkers inside sent the beast back under the water, and we watched it disappear into the dark depths once more. Smoke belched from our torn hull, out into the night sky, as the flames licked the deck, sending soldiers fleeing for their lives.

"That's the way, man. Give him what for!" I cheered as the deck guns blasted from our escort frigate again.

Our *hoorahs* were short lived however when the beast resurfaced—this time alongside the Ironclads—and seemed to torpedo through them without even stopping to turn. All it took was a thrash of its tail, and the ships were capsizing like rubber ducks in a bathtub. The smaller boats disappeared in the beast's wake as the *Olympic* blasted her horn and changed course, heading South, away from the carnage unfolding. The blue flashes in the sky lit the slippery bugger up like an electric eel gliding elegantly through the water, and we all watched its dexterity with gut-wrenching awe.

The *Titanic*, now with the gaping hole burning in her starboard side, was listing to the right but still firing full steam ahead with the *Fearless* by her side. Above us, the Zeppelin warships circled, trying to locate the beast with searchlights. I watched on as the sea frothed and the bubbles emerged. This time it was the smaller of the sister ships, the *Olympic,* that was being attacked, as two large claws grappled with the ship's rudder. We watched on helplessly again as the ship tipped port, then starboard, until the large smokestacks tumbled into the frothing sea.

It truly was a horrific sight to behold, with the beast's scaly back emerging from the sea like the slippery cobbled streets of London on a winter's day, and its huge menacing claws gleaming under the moonlight like diamond tipped stalactites tearing chunks of panelling from the ship's outer protection. Pitiful echoes of the passengers' screams filled the night air as we reloaded our rifles and readied ourselves for the beast to return to the *Titanic*.

The *Olympic* quickly followed the same fate as the Ironclads as we stood there dumfounded, watching the beast disappeared under the waves. We could barely hear the screaming of those survivors left behind in the water, as we were still fleeing the opposite way and, instead of saving those poor souls, we just stood on with our heads hung low.

The *Titanic* was listing slightly, but still afloat. If the beast returned, we were surely done for. I had to think fast, needed to rearrange my men for maximum defence if we were to have any chance of saving the *Titanic*.

From the darkness, I heard the haunting rendition of "Abide with me" as the quartet began playing on the deck; a slow heart jerking violin rendition echoing above the cries for help, accompanied by those retched bagpipe players.

"What the deuces are they up to, Smithy? Stick a rifle in their hands for pity's sake, or they are of no use to us in the bloody fight!" says I, surveying their morbid faces as HMS *Fearless* returned by our starboard side.

"And get these damn boats in the water before those men freeze out there!" I pointed to the survivors bobbing in the oil slicks below.

We had lost our fleet in only ten minutes of mayhem, and I was beginning to wonder if the *Titanic* might take on too much ballast and follow, but then I guffawed at that thought.

Smithy nodded, the music stopping when he grabbed the violin players bow and snapped it in two, replacing the instrument with a Mauser rifle he had found next to one of the fallen casualties. The musician looked on with horror.

"Get yer arse over there, sonny!" screamed the Sergeant Major, pointing to where the beast was breaching the icy depths again, slowly lifting itself onto the deck of our ship. The band members yelled, scattering in terror, as one of the slimy legs slid over the edge like the monster was climbing an oak tree on Wimbledon Common.

"Feckless flouncing morons!" Smithy cursed, taking a knee, and reloaded his rifle.

HMS *Fearless* began firing salvos again as the night sky lit up in fiery explosions. Gunfire popped all around me but was having little effect on the demon clambering aboard as the *Fearless* fired off another volley of shots. I could smell the acrid stench of the gunpowder and cordite in the air as it wafted past me with each whistling salvo. Several flew over our heads and splashed down in the ocean opposite as the immense beast clambered over the handrail and began swiping without prejudice at my men.

"Captain Paxmore, we need to get up there!" Smithy shouted, pointing to the chimney as I snatched my Enfield and bounded up the stairwell to the four large belching stacks towering above.

"Well said," says I, impatiently sneering down my moustache at him. "Don't just stand there, Sergeant Major, let's get this blighter before he can do us any more damage!"

"But Swarley..." says he, but I was already

halfway up the stairs to be concerned with listening to Smithy's objections.

This wingless, dragon demon—this frozen dinosaur from beyond Tesla's electromagnetic contraption of terror—was now standing upright on the deck, almost as tall as the chimney stacks, and swatting handfuls of my men into the ocean.

I was reminded of one of Darwin's comical illustrations of the rock-hopping lizards he had encountered in the Galapagos Islands, as the abomination raised one foot and stood towering on the men below.

They had little chance, as the *Titanic* lurched in the water. The lifeboats swung free and splashed down as dozens of men fell from their positions into the icy void, but still the beast hung on, cradling the smokestack as if it were in the middle of a damn love tryst.

"It's trying to rip the ship apart!" one of my

men yelled below.

Six of my finest sharp shooters, including a fine smelling young Red Cross Jezebel with the quickest reloading action I had ever seen, had joined me below stack number three, and we all proceeded to fire upon the devil himself. She joined me by the chimney stack as we slung our rifles behind our backs and began climbing the maintenance ladder that ran the length of the huge cylinder.

"Good god, woman, what the devil do you think you are doing?" I stammered as the ship swayed, first to port and then violently to starboard. We fell against each other, and then against the resting platform, as we raised our rifles towards the abomination. Her uniform hat was pinned to her vibrant red hair, which hung in loose ringlets cascading onto her shoulder, and I was rather taken aback for a moment as I got another waft of her perfume.

"I'm just as 'andy with a rifle as you are, sir!" said she with a wink, steadying herself as the *Titanic* righted, before she fired off three shots in the blink of an eye. I didn't doubt the nurse's spunk for a moment and actually felt a curious stirring in my loins.

"Well," I blustered, "aim for the beast's damn eyes then, woman!" says I above the commotion, making sure the angelic soldier heard me. She nodded and took aim as I watched on, dumbfounded at the speed of which she reloaded her Enfield.

Quite the filly indeed.

HMS *Fearless* continued to rain her shells towards the Tesla demon as we watched the beast's claws obliterate the chimney stack that Smithy and the others hid behind. It tore the stack from the bolts holding it to the deck, lifting the funnel above its head to swat away the falling artillery shells. As we stared on disbelieving, the beast then flung the chimney stack towards the *Fearless* and hit the frigate square in the middle of its structure. The *Fearless* fired off one more volley of shells before the guns ceased and the control tower shuddered, exploding in a glorious fireball, causing the whole ship to list and begin capsizing into the icy sea.

I watched on aghast as a solitary figure emerged from the ship's deck and saluted us before the HMS *Fearless* disappeared under the oily fire now spreading in its wake.

"Hell and the devil confound me! That's Churchill!"

One of the shells exploded off *Titanic's* chimney stack number two as the remainder of the rounds struck the icy beast's shoulders. I fell forwards, stumbling over the handrail as I watched my red-headed warrior nurse fire off three rounds, each striking the beast in the face before it reached out and swatted at our vantage point. We tumbled together, but I lost my footing and almost flipped over the balustrade, yelling as we lurched toward the deck below.

I wasn't sure if I grabbed her, or she me, but we somehow found ourselves entwined, hanging over the platform as the beast stumbled.

"Damn you all the way back to hell!" I yelled at the beast as it roared in pain, toppling backwards onto the helpless soldiers on the deck below, clutching at its bloody head wounds.

I felt the *Titanic* lurch back to the starboard side again as we floundered, arms flailing as we hung from the platform looking for a solid hand hold to grab onto. But as the beast stumbled backwards onto the stern deck, its shifting weight righted the ballast once more, and the *Titanic's* bow seemed to raise back up from the icy waters, sending us crashing back against the chimney stack's metal ladder as a huge tidal wave crashed into the floating wreckage below. I watched the life rafts capsize as I hung onto the nurse's back for dear life, staring at the pandemonium below like Captain Ahab, in disbelief.

I stared down into the abyss at the huge beastly carcass draped over the stern of the ship— its arms flapping over the port side and its legs over the starboard. The blood oozing from the demon's gills drained onto the deck as if we had been out with the Eskimos on a harpooning day out and caught our very own Moby Dick.

"Hold on, sir, I've got us!" my red-headed goddess exclaimed as she pulled us to safety.

Around us, sinking ships burned and Zeppelins circled, looking for survivors in the darkness as the sky flickered its alien blue aurora. Survivors screamed as rifle shots continued to crack into the chill of the evening.

I looked on in utter bewilderment and realised that the gates of hell had been unlatched by that madman Tesla.

But who was going to be the person to close the gate again?

Certainly not me, I realised, as I hung onto the nurse for dear life like a baby chimpanzee suckling on its mother's back.

Oh, but her red hair smelt so fine…

We entered the upper New York Bay four days later under the escort of the three remaining frigates from Roosevelt's Asiatic fleet. They had suffered the same heavy losses by similar demonic beasts crossing the Atlantic Ocean and were barely seaworthy now. Our Zeppelins, on request, had flown ahead with the king to rendezvous with President Roosevelt at the Garden City Aerodrome on Long Island, while we continued our journey to New York.

We did, however, continue to lumber the deceased beast on our deck after several failed attempts to blow the bugger to kingdom come, concluding it wiser to use the weight as ballast to refrain from taking on board any further water. So, our journey was considerably slower due to this troublesome inconvenience.

This fortuitous predicament allowed me more time to get acquainted with my new squeeze, Nurse Nancy, below deck, who it seemed had some rather fine tricks up her sleeve having not long returned from a trip to the Philippine Islands. What that woman could do with a loofah sponge and a bar of carbolic soap would shock the socks clean off any rapscallion I knew down the local boozer.

The *Titanic*'s captain had his orders to sail into the bay and disembark each Regiment onto the docks, but as each one of the ships passed under the watchful eye of madam Liberty—which was now just a frightening roosting porch for the sleeping demons huddled along her tainted hellish structure—

it was clear to see that we were steaming full speed into another frightful nightmare.

"Good God!" was all Smithy could manage, choking on a mouthful of brandy as we peered through the eerie fog blanketing the bay. But there was nothing good about what I was witnessing, for it was surely the devil's hands that had been busy in the bay.

Uncontained fires could be seen burning along the length of the industrial side of the city, while the familiar sound of mortar fire mingled with the cries of a city being smothered by death itself. Above, the skies seemed to squirm with the shroud of a thousand winged carriers of chaos, circling the Manhattan skyline in victory.

It was as if we had sailed straight into Dante's eighth layer of hell, and I have to admit that in a moment of weakness, I actually wondered *what if* the *Titanic* had just sunk out there in the middle of the

Atlantic Ocean? *What if* the band had played on as we just gave up and never survived to witness any of this apocalyptic nightmare?

I shuddered at this morbid thought.

Slumped ranks of thousands of dead bodies bobbed in the rancid waves below, floating forgotten amongst the twisted wreckage of broken contraptions, while the port bells rang out, warning us of the capsized boats that smouldered near the docklands.

Overhead, in the alien green hue of the sky, we heard the screeching of those damned creatures as a few began to dive towards the frigate now taking lead of the convoy.

Smithy wiped his chin and handed me back the brandy flask, and I took several large gulps of the liquor to steady my nerves.

"Tell our ship's captain to turn her around immediately, Smithy," says I as I watched the lead

American vessel steer onward into the fog.

"I don't like this predicament one little bit!" I turned, gesticulating to Smithy to sort out the men.

"Okay, lads, you know the drill." Smithy stood on a makeshift podium to give the men their orders.

"Let's no' have any fuckery now, Corporal Whitmore. I want guns mounted along the starboard deck and teams forward and aft!" There was a groan from those heading aft. Smithy had made the men dig foxholes into the belly of the beast laying across the rear of the ship, as its scales made for damn fine protection.

"Ha! And you thought it smelt bad on the outside!" says he, urging his men onward.

The stench *was* overbearing, but he assured our men they would be safer firing from those fleshy fox holes than simply to have each of them laying out on the deck.

To the east, we heard the familiar drone of our

Zeppelin squadron flying from the Long Island emerald smog, although now the squadron seemed rather depleted as it neared. My squinting eyes could only make out four dirigible airships heading our way, being followed by six winged demons…flying in perfect arrowhead formation!

It seemed the Zeppelins were being escorted to the *Titanic* by those creatures, three on each side of the formation.

"Satins breath!" I was unable to contain my astonishment at the sight unfolding. "Steady men, take aim!" I ordered, feeling the ship lurch as she turned.

"Sergeant Major, my eye scope, if it does you my good man!" Smithy recovered the instrument from my haversack and placed it in my hand, returning his thoughts to his Enfield, while I extended the scope and raised it to the formation above me.

"What madness is this?"

I could hardly believe what I was seeing. Indeed, I had to clear my eye several times to make sure I was not in some state of hallucinatory shock, influenced by the brandy.

Riding aloft each of the winged demons were soldiers dressed in leather protective suits and wearing flying goggles. Each rider carried what looked like long electrical cattle prods, crackling at the tips, while each of the demons was fitted with a riding harness, with bulky electrical apparatus buckled to their necks and prongs attached to their hideous heads. They fought furiously against their reins, but I watched the riders tame the beasts with the electrical rods sharply prodding into their sides as if they were jockeys riding troublesome mounts, galloping for the finish line.

A rifle shot cracked from the deck beside me, and I had to steady Smithy's aim.

"Hold your fire, man!" says I, handing my eye scope over to him in utter bewilderment.

"HOLD YOUR FIRE!" I turned, repeating the order louder as it reverberated down the line of confused soldiers.

As the riders and their mounts flew closer, I could make out the red, white and blue flapping canvas of the Old Glory flag draped behind each of the creatures.

I was about to meet President Theodore Roosevelt and his infamous Rough Riders.

Two of the flying beasts landed on the forward deck as another flapped its immense wings and perched upon one of the two chimney stacks that remained upright. The rest of the creatures circled the *Titanic,* along with the Zeppelins, and I watched as the first Rider dismounted and nodded my way. I instantly recognised him; what with his round rimmed spectacles and his pistol strapped to his thigh like some gunslinger of old.

"Mr President, sir!" says I.

"Captain Paxbrough," he replied.

"Paxmore, sir!" I corrected.

He returned my salute as he stepped from the beast, handing over the reins to one of his leather-clad soldiers mounted beside him, and I watched as he patted the creature's neck as if it were a stallion he had just galloped across an open pasture with.

"Such magnificent creatures, wouldn't you agree, Paxbrough?" He actually smiled as he walked over the deck to where Smithy and I stood, tipping his hat to those staring on.

"Magnificent is not a word I would use to describe something as grotesque as these demons from hell, Mr President, sir," says I, rather taken aback by the whole affair.

"Nonsense, Paxbrough, they just need a little bit of American persuasion is all. These are damn fine beasts, if you ask me. Once they are broken, they succumb like every other animal on the planet." He outstretched his hand, and I shook it firmly.

"In fact, I'm rather counting on you to fly back

with me to Long Island where you can pick up your own mount to lead your men in the charge."

"The charge?" says I. "What exactly are we charging, sir?"

Roosevelt turned, removed his heavy gloves, and pointed them towards the Long Island shoreline.

"The charge, Paxbrough. Over there." He placed a sweaty palm on my shoulder. His mount screeched and flapped its great wings as the soldier struggled to rein the beast in. My men were getting itchy trigger fingers at the sight of these creatures being on board the *Titanic*.

"I have twelve thousand men currently circling the wagons over there, eagerly awaiting your king's military might. I believe you have another ten thousand troops ready to fight alongside them to vanquish our enemy."

"Seven," I corrected.

"Say what?" Roosevelt replied, cleaning his

glasses.

"Seven thousand men, sir. We lost some fine fellows wrestling that blighter!" says I, pointing behind us to the carcass of the serpent sprawled over *Titanic's* hull.

"Ah yes, terrible business, but it's all in hand now I understand?" He gestured with his gloves again. "May I?"

"Be my guest, sir, although I must warn you; the smell is rather pungent," says I.

Roosevelt turned, and we began walking towards the aft of the ship. "Yes, they sure do stink the place up. I must admit, our goddamned camp is like an abattoir over there. Tell me, Swarley…can I call you Swarley?" I nodded, surprised he'd managed to remember my name at last. "Swarley, what do you know of Tesla and his work?"

"Nikola Tesla?" says I.

"Yes, the scientist," Roosevelt replied as

Smithy cleared the way ahead. The grubby soldiers jostled for a glimpse of the leader but made no attempt to interrupt.

"Well, sir, I think the man is a buffoon to think he could subject us all to damnation with his experiments without the foresight of errors such as these." I pointed to the circling beasts above Manhattan.

"I mean, what the devil did that imbecile think he was going to achieve with this contraption of his anyway? Give away free electricity to all? Not much of a capitalist thing to do for his country now is it, Mr President?" I guffawed as Roosevelt nodded thoughtfully.

"Yes, well, the man sure does have some rather amusing ideas in his head." Roosevelt stopped in his tracks and stared up at the slain water dragon on our deck. "Lord almighty, what an absolutely astonishing specimen."

I turned to see Nurse Nancy at the doorway, winking at me—the saucy mare. "Yes, she is rather a splendid catch, sir," says I, leaning over to him, "and rather agile in the sack too, I might add."

Roosevelt turned, ignoring my rather embarrassing faux pas as he stood gazing at the beast before him. But Nancy did give my rear a subtle grope as I passed her.

"You see, Swarley, this is what I am talking about. Tesla has invented a doorway to another realm, allowing creatures like these to come knocking. And I want to have control of those who visit." He turned to me like some demented war lord. "Tesla has worked on a way to control these creatures with the help of some tinkering of the brainwaves and the aid of electrolysis. If we can control the doorway, we can control those that pass through it. So what if there has been a slight problem in the teething department. A small oversight."

"A small oversight!" says I, but he held up a finger to halt my interruption.

"Swarley, I am counting on men like you to command your fine men and lead this charge, because I'm sure we can take back control of Wardenclyffe and reclaim Nikola Tesla's groundbreaking work. Think of the power we would have if we had an army of these creatures to police the world. We…along with our allies, of course…would surely be invincible."

I was looking at the face of a madman. He wanted to tame these creatures, to create an army. The same creatures that had levelled half of England and most of Manhattan.

"Are you suggesting that we capture these demons, sir?" says I, rubbing my neck in confusion.

"No, Swarley, not the demons themselves. We need to take back the doorway Tesla opened up on Wardenclyffe, and then corral the beasts."

"I'm not sure I understand correctly, sir, what exactly is waiting for us at Wardenclyffe?" says I, unsure what it was I and my men were actually recruited to do for Roosevelt.

"Nikola Tesla built his electroconductor tower on the cliffs of Wardenclyffe. It links all the other towers together to create his worldwide web of free intercontinental electrical power for all to use. It is the conduit for all towers to be controlled." He stared at me with those wide eyes of his. "We are going to take back control of his laboratory!"

I laughed at this, much to the bemusement of Roosevelt, who pulled out a small device from his pocket and signalled to the Zeppelins above with the aid of this contraption I had never set eyes on before.

"Tesla!" Roosevelt shouted into the contraption.

"Yes, sir?" A voice crackled from the handheld device.

"Release the cage!"

I watched as one of the Zeppelins above slowed and steadied at the *Titanic's* bow.

"You, sir, are in for one fine doozy of a treat!"

I followed Roosevelt to the front of the *Titanic,* where I watched a large cage being lowered onto the deck. This was quite a feat, as the *Titanic* was still contouring the Long Island coastline.

"It's called a Faraday cage!" Roosevelt shouted over the winch's turbine. "Tesla informs me he will be protected from the electromagnetic forces given off by the Tesla's coil. A most spectacular invention, wouldn't you agree, Swarley?"

I could only stare at the meshed box in awe; I had seen nothing like it in all my forty-eight years.

"And the harpoon gun?" says I, looking at the massive weapon poking from the cage as it spun slowly around above the deck.

"Ah, that. That is the thing that is going to win

us back our tower," Roosevelt replied. "We need to get this ship close enough to the Wardenclyffe laboratory for Tesla to fire off the harpoon bolt into the structure and earth the massive voltage it's producing, dissipating the current into the sea." He nodded as he spoke. "It's all very scientific!"

"Say what?" I had no idea what the man was babbling about.

"The spools of copper cable you see being loaded will allow the current to flow from Tesla's coil perched on top of Wardenclyffe Tower, and down into the sea where it will dissipate, allowing you and your men to charge the laboratory and seize control of the equipment."

"And what if the harpoon fails to discharge the voltage into the sea, Mr Roosevelt, sir? What then?" I was beginning to wish I had never left Liverpool.

"Well then, Swarley, I'm afraid both you and I will fry a most horrendous death on the battlefield, sir. There is no other option if we are to defend this great nation!"

The president slapped me on the shoulder as the cage finally slammed onto the *Titanic*'s deck.

"Here's the very man now who will be manning the harpoon!"

The cage door swung open, and out sprang Nikola Tesla himself with his hand outstretched.

"Mr Paxmore, it is both an honour and a privilege to meet you, sir!"

Smithy informed me I was lucky not to find myself in the ship's brig after gifting Tesla a rather fine uppercut, causing him a fat lip. It seemed Roosevelt had a sense of humour though and merely held me back before I could do any further injury to the madman who had been the cause of many of my men's demise. I did, however, tell the bugger to go toast his bloomin' eyebrows before we left him to bastardise the *Titanic*.

But later, as I stared down from the leather saddle of my very own dragon—Swarley Paxmore and his Dragon Dragoon Guard…it has a certain regal madness to it—and watched the *Titanic* leaving the port, I began to wonder who the madman actually was.

Smithy had taken the lead below on Betsy—after promising to take good care of my mount. He flanked the ground units, barking out instructions, while I reluctantly had taken to the air in formation behind Roosevelt and his own Rough Riders, awaiting the order to strike.

The *Titanic*, now steaming ahead up the coastline, had been refitted with the harpoon gun by a rather angry Nikola Tesla, who was quite insistent that he and his lab technicians make some modifications to the vessel's deck, winding lengths of electrical copper coils around her entire front deck, before they set sail around Long Island.

Tesla said it was merely for protection, nothing more. But I watched that fraudster and his team attaching rings of copper wiring around the *Titanic* all day, fine tuning his cage, and measuring distances with oscilloscopes and trundle wheels. He was up to something for sure—perhaps installing a new electronic weapon to defeat the beasts—but I hadn't the foggiest idea what.

The rest of the men awaiting orders by the dock had been fed and armed and were now being escorted by Roosevelt's ground forces, gaining ground on Wardenclyffe Tower quickly. I saw the flags of several other nations being flown ahead of the men, horses readying for the charge.

Even the bloody French were ranking alongside the sergeant major, who was now under orders to lead our men straight to Tesla's laboratory, while I, and several dozens of Roosevelt's Rough Riders, would divert as much of the unwanted demon attention from the front line and initiate a bloody sky battle above the coastline.

The odds were ridiculously mounted against us,

not to mention it being my first time riding into battle on the back of a bloody dragon!

"This is utter madness, Teddy!" says I as my dragon bucked me like a rodeo clown in the ring. The wind was howling around my face as I readjusted myself on the beast's back. Roosevelt laughed, pointing down at the *Titanic*.

"Not as mad as that genius, Tesla. Look!" says he, as the *Titanic* veered towards the laboratory situated on the cliff wall.

"Come on, Paxbrough, let's take a closer gander before it starts getting crowded up here," Roosevelt shouted, banking off to the left and dive-bombing the coastline as the beasts circling the tower began breaking formation and heading our way. I watched the damn show off as he grabbed his hat, screaming out, and dug his spurs into his mount's belly like he was screaming Wild Bill Hickok.

I lost Roosevelt soon after we entered a swarm

of demons that engulfed the entire squadron of Rough Riders, separating us. During the melee, my dragon wasn't attacked once, but I was buffeted around like a groom strapped to a chair at a Jewish circle dance—most likely due to my fear of falling off, and my complete lack of control of the beast. I merely held on tight around its neck, a helpless passenger, watching on aghast as my dragon obliterated Roosevelt's Rough Riders one by one.

"Use the damn rod, Paxbrough!" I heard one rider shout out before he was torn from his dragon and sent spinning to the ground troops below who were approaching the compound that was being fiercely guarded by the creatures.

I could only imagine how Smithy was feeling as he charged headlong into those snapping mouthfuls of prehistoric teeth that had ripped apart so many of our men in Blackpool.

The Zeppelins ahead were firing rapid machine

gun belts through the green haze at us, and I watched as the creatures shrieked and clawed at the skies with talons like Japanese ceremonial swords. They had little chance against the modern chain guns, or at least that's what I thought until one of the blighters tumbled straight through the command module with claws out and engulfed the poor beggars inside in an almighty helium explosion. What was left of the Zeppelin plunged to the ground, trailing ribbons of smoke and flames.

I hoped for the sake of England that the king was not aboard that stricken Zeppelin.

The *Titanic,* by this time, had picked up maximum knots as it rammed its way towards the coastline, lurching as it ran aground against the shallow waters under the cliff. The captain blew her steam whistle, crunching her bow headlong into the cliffs as boulders the size of carriages crashed down on the wooden deck around Tesla. This time it was the metal hull screeching against the rocks that tore the panelling below deck; buckling and twisting as she ground to a sudden halt, marooning herself upon that beach as her defiant horn bellowed.

I was in the battle of my life, just trying to keep my dragon from attacking my own side, trying desperately to watch the carnage below as the damn thing resisted the constant zapping of the cattle prod in my hand.

How in God's name was I supposed to fight these demons when this damned jackass of a beast wouldn't get us back into the battle? For all I knew, Roosevelt was still up there leading the charge and awaiting my arrival.

We both shrieked as we nosedived the *Titanic*, him snapping and gnawing at the metal riding bit covered in putrid saliva foaming between his teeth, and me cursing the infernal devil for not adhering to a single command I gave it. It was like riding a damn unicycle while sat on a seat made from hot pokers up my hairy jacksy. My arms ached and my thighs strained against the belly of the beast, my leather binds squeezing tighter than a Brigadier's wife's girdle during judging of a garden fete homemade cake competition.

Tesla was battling against his own beasts as they swooped the deck and clattered against the large metal Faraday cage he was now locked inside of. I wondered just how close he needed to be before he shot the harpoon contraption at his electrical tower and earthed the voltage into the sea. But I had little time to ponder this thought, as my mount twisted between the *Titanic*'s remaining chimney stacks and shot straight through the swooping demons barrelling high into the glowing night sky.

Wardenclyffe Tower glowed, alive with the crackling of a million volts coursing through the spherical coil mounted on the top of the structure. I could feel the hairs on my neck stand to attention and my teeth vibrating as we swooped around the monolith that was now emitting huge electrical bolts of discharge that struck the fields between the approaching cavalry. More of the flying beasts joined the aerial fight as Roosevelt and several of his Rough Riders sliced through a pack of the ferocious demons, engulfed by the blue crackle of lightning bolts. I was so dizzy, I could barely keep my eyes from crossing with all the looping and barrelling my dragon was doing, having as much input into the battle as a soggy paper kite cut free of its tether during a rainstorm.

My anger got the better of me, and I thrust the electric cattle prod device deep into the damned thing's side, cursing to the heavens.

"ENOUGH! Enough of this you wretched spawn of Satan!" To which the beast actually screeched, then settled and began taking my harness commands.

"Now that is much more civil," says I as the creature relented and steadied, gliding above the pasture towards the stampeding horsemen heading my way.

Good old Smithy was charging straight for the laboratory, awaiting the imminent order to strike from the *Titanic*. Only now, it was I who was in the way of six hundred pounding hooves, perched awkwardly on top of a dragon who was now stubbornly ignoring its orders once more.

"Bugger me with a pitchfork!" says I, straining with all my might to pull the beast up, but the damned creature was having none of it. Instead, it veered straight into the advancing cavalry flank.

To my horror, I found myself bowling down my own screaming men like pins on a skittle board. The damn beast roared and screeched with each slice of the swords glinting in the melee, while I held on to its neck for dear life.

In amongst the commotion, a huge cheer went up as an immense explosion blasted me from behind, and I turned to see the tower being rocked by a single harpoon fired from the *Titanic* below.

Lightning bolts shuddered in the sky, engulfing the battlefield in blinding blue light as both demons and Zeppelins fell from the sky. I pulled my reins with all my strength and managed to avoid hitting any more of the blinded soldiers now sprinting towards the laboratory that the tower stood upon.

But my dragon was done for.

The broken beast pitched and rolled towards the earth, striking the ground hard and snapping its neck, and I was launched from the leather blood-soaked saddle and hurtled towards the cliff edge.

The brightest of electrifying light engulfed us all…and then darkness followed.

I opened my eyes wearily and lifted my head from the burnt grass, spitting out teeth and blood, and realised the humming had stopped, although my remaining teeth still rattled in my gums.

All was still, even the lightning bolts terrorising the night sky had gone.

An uneasy quietness blanketed the killing ground where the raging battle of gunfire and torment had played out only moments earlier.

No screams came from the unconscious men now lying scattered in the surrounding fields.

No screeching came from the beasts that had

been blinded by the light as they tumbled from the sky, hitting the ground hard in mounds of broken wings.

Only the sound of the waves crashing against the cliff wall below (and the slight ringing of tinnitus in my ears) could be heard.

The tower was silent. No demons from another realm circled the sky above. No cavalry charged towards the tower. No Zeppelins hovered above.

"Smithy?" called I, turning my head to view the battlefield.

The eerie green mist had descended from the sky and hung around the battlefield like drifting cannon smoke across no-man's-land, and as I slowly got to my knees, wiping down my tunic, I could hear the groans of other men awakening.

The slight burnt smell of the dusty electrical storm wafted up from the sea below, and I peered over the cliff edge in astonishment, blinking away what I thought was dirt in my eyes.

When I opened them again, I could see the faintest flickering outline of the *Titanic,* lingering like the dying filament in a lightbulb. She sat on the rippling water like a ghost; her buckled front end wedged into the cliff face, dissolving like a forgotten thought on the tip of one's tongue and then reappearing.

A phantom ship.

I was sure I could see a figure standing on deck as I watched; slack jawed. Then, in the blink of an eye, the *Titanic* was gone.

Another one of Tesla's heinous electrical experiments, no doubt.

Behind me, I could hear rifle fire and the clanging of swords upon dragon scales as the fighting commenced once more; heroic cavalry men fighting demons with broken wings; horses braying as they galloped my way in the panic of battle; the sound of the bugle calling survivors to arms.

It was Betsy that caught my eye, her rider unseated during battle, she now galloped my way.

"Now, now, Betsy!" says I, realising that Smithy was missing. She slowed and snorted beside me with her reins dragging in the grass. I gave her a gentle rub on the nose, then mounted her and turned her back to the battlefield.

"FOR KING AND COUNTRY!" says I, raising my regimental sabre.

And why the hell wouldn't I?

Roosevelt's damn war has been won, but the wretched Battle for Wardenclyffe still raged on.

Besides, I still have dragons to slay.

ABOUT THE AUTHOR

GREGG CUNNINGHAM is a multi-genre short story writer from Western Australia.

He's had stories published by 559 Publishing in *13 Bites*: Volume 3, 4 and 5, *Plan 559 from Outer Space:* Volume 2 and 3, *Other Realms*, *Heard It on the Radio* and *559 Ways to Die*.

He has also had several stories published by Zombie Pirate Publishing in *Relationship Add Vice*, *Full Metal Horror*, *Phuket Tattoo*, *World War Four*, *Flash Fiction Addiction* and *Grievous Bodily Harm*.

He hopes to one day dust down and edit the huge manuscript under his bed and get it out to the Sci-Fi community.

Bibliography

ANGELS, Black Hare Press, 2019

BEYOND, Black Hare Press, 2019

Deep Space, Black Hare Press, 2019

MONSTERS, Black Hare Press, 2019

Storming Area 51, Black Hare Press, 2019

WORLDS, Black Hare Press, 2019

WARDENCLYFFE, Black Hare Press, 2020

Connect

Twitter: *@GGGcunningham*

Website: *cortlandsdogs.wordpress.com*

ABOUT THE PUBLISHER

BLACK HARE PRESS is a small, independent publisher based in Melbourne, Australia.

Founded in 2018, our aim has always been to champion emerging authors from all around the globe and offer opportunities for them to participate in speculative fiction and horror short story anthologies.

Connect

Website: *www.blackharepress.com*

Twitter: *@BlackHarePress*

GREGG CUNNINGHAM

www.ingramcontent.com/pod-product-compliance
Lightning Source LLC
Chambersburg PA
CBHW030648190726

48286CB00008B/2721